The Dragonsitter in the Land of the Dragons

First published in 2019 by
Andersen Press Limited
20 Vauxhall Bridge Road
London SW1V 2SA
www.andersenpress.co.uk

2 4 6 8 10 9 7 5 3 1

British Library Cataloguing in Publication Data available.

ISBN 978 1 78344 800 5

This book is printed on FSC accredited paper from responsible sources.

Printed and bound in Great Britain by
Clays Limited, Elcograf S.p.A.

The Dragonsitter in the Land of the Dragons

Josh Lacey

Illustrated by Garry Parsons

Andersen Press
London

Dear Mum

I have to tell you something.

I am not in Glasgow with Uncle Morton.

We are actually a bit further away.

In fact we are four thousand, three hundred and twenty-nine miles further away.

I know we said we were going to Glasgow for the weekend to buy a new washing machine, but that wasn't exactly true. Instead we went to the airport and got on a plane to Mongolia.

I hope you don't mind.

Uncle Morton thought you would like to have some special time with the baby.

Also Gordon is always saying he needs a quiet day in the new house to do some serious DIY, and this could be the perfect opportunity.

You'll just have to ask Emily to keep out of his way.

We arrived in Ulaanbaatar this afternoon.

We had to spend ages in customs because the officials were very suspicious of our luggage. They couldn't understand why we needed so much chocolate. Finally Uncle Morton gave them two boxes of Maltesers and they let us through.

So far, Mongolia is nice. Our hotel is cosy. We're having delicious dim sum in the hotel restaurant. Then we need to find someone to drive us to the mountains tomorrow.

When we get there, we're going to watch the Great Dragon Battle Ceremony with Uncle Morton's old friend Professor Baast. Apparently this is a once-in-a-lifetime opportunity, so I didn't want to miss it.

We should be back in a week or two.

Love from

Eddie

Hi Eddie

Ha ha ha!

Mum xx

PS How did you and Morton make those photos of Mongolia look so realistic?

Dear Mum

I'm not joking.

Actually I had forgotten it was even April Fools' Day today.

I really am in Mongolia.

Uncle Morton says didn't you get his message? He popped a note through the front door, explaining everything.

He says he might have got the wrong door, because he's only been to our new house twice, so maybe you should ask the neighbours.

Everything is fine here. We spent the whole day driving. Now we're staying in another hotel.

This one isn't as nice as the one in Ulaanbaatar. The food in the restaurant was horrid. I asked Uncle Morton if I could eat some of our chocolate, but he said we've got to save it all for the dragons.

There is one good thing about this hotel: our room has a brilliant view of the mountains. Tomorrow we are going to drive up there and look for Professor Baast.

Uncle Morton had a message from him three days ago, saying the Great Dragon Battle Ceremony would be starting any minute now. Apparently he's found a cave in the mountains which is the perfect place to watch the ceremony from.

Unfortunately, Professor Baast didn't say exactly where this cave is, but we're going to go and look for it.

Love from

Eddie

From: Mum

To: Edward Smith-Pickle

Date: Monday 2 April

Subject: No more fooling

 Attachments: Meg

Hi Eddie

Don't you know April Fools are meant to stop at midday on the 1st?

Please don't send me any more silly emails. Or fake photos. Just come home.

I didn't get any messages from Morton.

In fact, I have rung him about ten times, but he isn't answering his phone.

Are you hiding on his island? If so, please ask him to bring you straight home in his boat.

We are all missing you. Emily says the house is much too quiet without you here. And baby Meg is miserable without her favourite big brother. She keeps looking around and making funny little noises.

If she could talk, I'm sure she would be saying, "Where's Eddie?"

We're having spaghetti bolognese for supper tonight. I'll make it with extra tomato, just how you like it.

See you later.

Love from

Mum xx

From: Edward Smith-Pickle

To: Mum

Date: Monday 2 April

Subject: Spaghetti

 Attachments: Our hosts

Dear Mum

Your message made me feel so hungry!

Right now, there is nothing I would like more than a big plate of spaghetti bolognese with lots of grated cheese.

Unfortunately I can't come home and eat it, because I am four thousand miles away.

I know you're worried about me, but you really don't have to be. Mongolia is very nice.

Today we drove to the end of the road.

It really was the end of the road.

The road went higher and higher into the mountains, then stopped in the middle of a field. The taxi had to turn around because it couldn't go any further.

We walked to the nearest village, which took about three hours. When we arrived, the villagers all came out of their houses to stare at us. The little children reached out their hands to touch me as if they didn't believe I was real. Uncle Morton said they had probably never seen a foreigner before.

We are staying the night with a very friendly family. There's a mum and a dad and six children. They're all going to sleep in one bed and we're going to sleep in the other.

For supper we had zblg, which is a famous local delicacy made from a special bit of a sheep. I asked Uncle Morton which bit, but he said it would be better if I didn't know.

I can tell you one thing about zblg. Spaghetti bolognese is a lot nicer.

The villagers said Professor Baast came through this village two weeks ago, but they haven't seen him since. Tomorrow we're going to hire some horses and follow his route into the mountains.

I just hope we don't miss the Great Dragon Battle Ceremony.

Love from

Eddie

Eddie

This isn't funny any more.

To be honest, it wasn't very funny in the first place.

As you can probably imagine, I'm really not in the mood for jokes. I have a three-month-old baby to look after, not to mention a new house to furnish and decorate. So please stop messing around and be serious for a moment.

Where are you?

We have just taken the boat to Morton's island, and there was no sign of you. Or my brother. His post hasn't been collected. His two dragons were sitting outside the front door, looking thoroughly miserable.

Luckily we had brought some chocolate.
After a Twix each and several packets of
Maltesers, Ziggy and Arthur both seemed
a bit more cheerful. But I think they would
be much happier if Morton came home and
took proper care of them.

I have tried ringing him about a hundred
times, but he never answers his phone.

Please ask him to ring me immediately.
Or call me yourself.

Mum

From: Edward Smith–Pickle

To: Mum

Date: Tuesday 3 April

Subject: Bob

Attachments: Bob; Bob's best friend

Dear Mum

I just tried to call you, but the phone doesn't seem to be working. Uncle Morton says we don't have a good signal because the mountains get in the way.

I'll try again tomorrow when we're a bit higher up.

I'm sorry to hear about Ziggy and Arthur. Perhaps you could dragonsit them till we're back? You wouldn't have to worry about them messing up the house, because Gordon hasn't even painted it yet.

Everything is fine here. We have spent the whole day riding up the mountain. Now we are literally in the middle of nowhere.

Luckily we have a guide to show us where to go.

He told me his name about twenty times, but I just can't pronounce it correctly. So Uncle Morton suggested I should call him Bob.

Bob can't pronounce my name either, so we're quits.

He is a tall man with big hands and a long droopy moustache.

He asked why we wanted to go to the mountains. Uncle Morton said it was because we just love being high up.

Bob twirled the ends of his moustache
and said something in his own language.
Later Uncle Morton told me it meant, "All
foreigners are crazy."

We have also hired three horses and a camel.

The three of us are riding the horses
and the camel is carrying our luggage.

This picture of the camel is for Emily. I hope
she likes it.

Love from

Eddie

Dear Eddie

Please tell Morton that I have been in contact with the police.

They confirmed that you and Morton flew from Glasgow to Ulaanbaatar. So now I know you weren't joking.

I wish you had been.

The police have promised to contact their colleagues in Mongolia. If they find your uncle, they will arrest him immediately, and throw him in jail.

I'm sure you don't want that to happen. I'm sure he doesn't either. So please ask him to take you straight to the nearest airport and put you on the first plane back to Scotland.

Mum

Dear Mum

You really don't have to worry about me. I'm very safe. I've only fallen off the horse once, and it didn't even hurt.

We've been riding higher and higher into the mountains. The air is very cold here. It's lucky you bought me those new jumpers for Christmas, because I'm wearing all three.

We passed a big patch of snow on the ground. I wanted to make a snowman, but Uncle Morton said there wasn't time. Finding Professor Baast is taking longer than we thought.

Uncle Morton says he can't be far away. I just hope we catch up with him before the Great Dragon Battle Ceremony finishes.

Did Emily like the picture of the camel?

Love from

Eddie

From: Mum

To: Edward Smith-Pickle

Date: Thursday 5 April

Subject: Come home!

Dear Eddie

I'm so worried about you. You're not old enough to go to the shops on your own, let alone Outer Mongolia.

What on earth are you even doing there? What is the Great Dragon Battle Ceremony? It sounds extremely dangerous.

I wish you'd come home.

Your uncle is utterly selfish. He was a selfish little boy when he and I were growing up together, many years ago, and he is just as selfish today.

But you're not like him, Eddie.

You're thoughtful, sensible, and kind. You always have been.

I know we've been through a lot of changes recently. Moving to Scotland. The new house. The new baby. It must have been difficult for you.

Perhaps Gordon and I have been so busy that we haven't paid enough attention to you. Is that how you feel? If so, I'm very sorry, and we'll try to do better in the future.

We love you, Eddie. We just want you to be happy. And safe.

So please come home.

Mum

Dear Mum

You don't have to worry. I like our new house. I like Meg too. I am happy.

I just wanted to see the Great Dragon Battle Ceremony.

You really don't have to worry about me being safe. I am looking after myself very well. Uncle Morton is looking after me too. And Bob is looking after both of us, and the horses, and the camel. We're all going to be fine.

Tonight we're staying in another village. They were very excited to meet foreigners. Bob told them that we had come all the way from Scotland, so they cooked us a special dinner. They made zblg.

24

Uncle Morton ate my portion as well as his. He said I should learn to appreciate the cuisines of different cultures.

I said I do appreciate the cuisines of different cultures. Spaghetti bolognese is my favourite food, and it comes from Italy.

I just don't like zblg.

The villagers opened a big bottle of their local drink. Uncle Morton let me have one glass. He said I should drink it all in one go. Luckily I just tried a tiny sip. It was so disgusting I had to spit it out in my zblg.

Uncle Morton says if you want to learn about the Great Dragon Battle Ceremony, you just need to search on the internet, and you'll find lots of information.

I've been trying to call you all day, but the phone doesn't seem to be working. I'll try again tomorrow.

Love from

Eddie

Dear Eddie

I have been calling Morton's phone all day, but I haven't managed to get through. Please do call me back. I'm desperate to talk to you.

Emily, Meg and I went back to your uncle's island this afternoon. The dragons are still looking miserable. Arthur only ate half the bar of milk chocolate that we gave him, and Ziggy wouldn't even touch her Mars bar. She just opened one eye, looked at us for a moment, then closed it again and went back to sleep.

Perhaps they're missing Morton.

We are certainly missing you.

I looked up the Great Dragon Battle Ceremony on the internet, and it all sounds extremely dangerous.

I hope it has finished before you get there.

Love from

Mum xx

The Great Dragon Battle Ceremony

Professor Ganbaataryn Baast
Translated from the Mongolian by Morton Pickle

Professor Ganbaataryn Baast

"No greater battle has ever been seen, no more beautiful dance has ever been witnessed." So says the old Mongolian proverb, describing the famous Great Dragon Battle Ceremony.

What is the meaning of the ceremony? Is it really a battle? If so, why are the dragons fighting? And what are they fighting for?

Wood carving, c. 1480, National Museum of Mongolia

Unfortunately, modern scholars cannot answer any of these questions, because none of us has ever witnessed the ceremony itself.

One fifteenth-century traveller describes a war between dragons so fierce that flames covered the entire sky. Another traveller, visiting the mountains in 1782, claims to have seen a dead dragon dropping from the sky.

We have no way of knowing if these are accurate reports or mere fantasy.

Ancient tales relate that the ceremony will take place only on a night when the moon is fresh, the sky is clear, the sun is warm, the snow is ready to melt, and Venus is in the ascendant. Such a date is almost certain to be in April, and so I have ventured to the mountains every spring for the past twenty-three years, hoping to witness the ceremony.

My patience has not yet been rewarded. But I will not give up until I see the Great Dragon Battle Ceremony with my own eyes.

Dear Mum

It was very nice to talk to you this morning.

I'm sorry you got so cross with Uncle Morton. Like I said, this whole thing really isn't his fault. I was the one who insisted on coming with him.

I will try to ring you again tomorrow.

We've been riding higher and higher into the mountains, but we had to stop this afternoon because it was snowing so hard. Now we're camping beside the path.

Bob wants to turn back.

He says this part of the mountains is very dangerous. There are ferocious flying beasts which eat anyone who comes near.

31

Every year, he says, they grab sheep from the hillsides, and they even steal children who wander too far from the villages.

But Uncle Morton and I aren't worried.

We have a rucksack stuffed with chocolate, which will be enough to make friends with even the most vicious and bloodthirsty dragon.

Love from

Eddie

From: Edward Smith-Pickle

To: Mum

Date: Sunday 8 April

Subject: Camping

Dear Mum

I have been trying to call you all day, but the phone doesn't seem to be working. I hope you get this message.

We have been riding from dawn till dusk. Now we're camping on another part of the mountainside. It's still snowing. I'm shivering so much I can hardly type.

Bob tried to light a fire to heat up the zblg, but the gas canister exploded, burning off his moustache. He put out the flames by rolling in the snow.

Supper was cold zblg, which is even worse than hot zblg. I asked Uncle Morton if I could have one tiny little piece of chocolate, but he said no. We have to keep it all for the dragons.

Eddie

Dear Mum

Bob has gone home. He said he doesn't want to be eaten by a dragon. He said we should go with him if we ever want to see our families again.

We tried to explain that dragons don't really eat people, but he wouldn't believe us.

He took the camel and two horses, but left us the third. It will carry our bags while we walk up the mountain.

I hope you're getting all these messages. I haven't had any back from you. Maybe the phone isn't working properly so high up in the mountains.

Love from

Eddie

Dear Mum

We walked all day and now we're camping in a beautiful spot on the side of the mountain.

The snow has finally stopped and we can see for miles.

Uncle Morton spotted a cave through his binoculars. He thinks that might be the cave that Professor Baast mentioned in his message. Tomorrow morning we'll walk up there and have a look.

Zblg for supper again.

Love from

Eddie

Dear Mum

We've found Professor Baast.

Or what was left of him, anyway. There wasn't much more than some chewed-up bones at the back of this cave.

The rest of him must have been eaten.

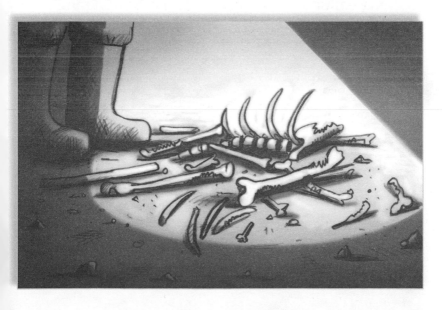

We don't know exactly what happened to him. Uncle Morton says he might have been attacked by wolves, eagles, or snow leopards. An expert would be able to tell by looking at the bite marks.

I've never seen Uncle Morton so upset.

He is burying the bones under a big pile of stones. Once he's finished, we're going to head back down the mountain.

We haven't seen the Great Dragon Battle Ceremony, but Uncle Morton says we shouldn't hang around in case the wolves, eagles, or snow leopards come back again.

So I shall see you quite soon.

Love from

Eddie

From: Edward Smith-Pickle
To: Mum
Date: Wednesday 11 April
Subject: URGENT!!!
Attachments: SOS

Dear Mum

As soon as you get this, please call the British Embassy in Ulaanbaatar ASAP and ask the Ambassador to rescue me.

That's what Uncle Morton said I should do in an emergency.

I think this probably counts as an emergency.

I am stuck in a cave with three enormous dragons. They've just eaten our horse and I'm worried they want me for pudding.

They must be the same ones who ate Professor Baast.

Uncle Morton is here with me, but he was knocked on the head by a dragon's tail and he's lying on the ground with his eyes closed. I can't make him wake up.

I have tried calling you, but the phone just says NETWORK UNAVAILABLE.

I hope you do get this. The dragons are looking hungry.

Eddie

From: Edward Smith–Pickle
To: Mum
Date: Wednesday 11 April
Subject: ALSO VERY URGENT!!!

Attachments: Eagle mountain; massive dragon

Dear Mum

I missed out an important piece of information in my last message. I didn't tell you where I am, which was pretty silly of me, because how will the Ambassador be able to come and rescue us if he doesn't know where I am?

The problem is, I don't actually know where I am.

You can tell the Ambassador we drove for two days from Ulaanbaatar, then travelled by horse and camel for five more days, and now we're near an enormous mountain which looks like an eagle's head. He'll probably be able to work it out.

Please ask him to be quick. Otherwise we're going to be eaten just like Professor Baast. And our horse.

I did try to tiptoe towards the cave's entrance. The nearest dragon lifted its neck and breathed a great gust of flames in my direction. I ran back to where I'd been sitting before.

Uncle Morton just woke up. I gave him the last of our water. He said, "Thank you, Caroline."

I told him I was actually Eddie, but he had already closed his eyes. Now he's asleep again.

I wish I knew what to do.

Luckily I've got the torch you gave me for my birthday or I'd be sitting here in the dark.

I'm shining it in the dragons' eyes. I hope it makes them uncomfortable.

Perhaps they'll decide to go and look for their next meal somewhere else.

Love from

Eddie

Dear Mum

The battery on my torch has run out already. If I ever get home, you should take it back to the shop and complain. I've hardly used it.

Apart from the torch, things are about the same as yesterday.

The dragons woke up at dawn. One of them stretched and another yawned. Then the biggest of them stared at me. Smoke trickled out of his nostrils.

I wanted to run away. But they were blocking the entrance.

The enormous dragon pulled himself to his feet and lumbered towards me.

I don't know if he wanted to eat me or Uncle Morton. Or both of us.

Luckily I didn't have to find out, because I remembered what we'd packed in our biggest rucksack.

I unwrapped a Crunchie and threw it in his direction.

He caught it in his mouth and swallowed it in one gulp. Then he banged his tail on the ground.

I don't think he'd ever tasted anything so delicious.

I threw him a Mars bar.

He liked that even more.

By this time, the other two dragons were on their feet too.

I gave them six Curly Wurlies and eleven bars of milk chocolate.

They ate the lot and went back to sleep.

I hope the Ambassador gets here before they wake up again.

Eddie

From: Edward Smith-Pickle

To: Mum

Date: Thursday 12 April

Subject: Goodbye

 Attachments: No escape

Dear Mum

This is just to say goodbye.

The dragons are getting restless and I can see the hunger in their eyes. Unfortunately I don't have any more chocolate. They've already eaten it all.

Please say goodbye to Emily from me.

And Dad.

And Gordon.

And Meg too, although she won't understand till she's older.

Uncle Morton asked me to say goodbye from him too.

He's woken up properly now, although he's still got a terrible headache.

He says he's very sorry. He wishes he'd never brought me here.

I wish he hadn't either.

I'd better go. The dragons are coming for us.

I'm going to try to fight them off with the torch. It's the only weapon I've got.

Love from

Eddie

Dear Mum

You don't have to worry. I'm still alive.
So is Uncle Morton.

It was close, though.

The three enormous dragons were literally
just about to eat us.

The biggest of them was advancing on me.
When he opened his mouth, I could see
all the way down his throat. Smoke curled
around his lips.

Suddenly there was a commotion in the
mouth of the cave and in flew two more
dragons. A big one and a small one.

For a horrible moment I thought they'd
come to eat us too.

Then I recognised them.

It was Ziggy and Arthur!

I've never been happier to see anyone in my whole life.

They are both much smaller than the dragon who was planning to eat me, but that didn't stop them. Ziggy charged straight at him. Arthur did too.

The big dragon sent a burst of flames
in their direction as if to say, "Leave me
alone, this boy is mine, I want to eat him all
myself."

Ziggy and Arthur breathed fire straight
back as if to say, "You can't eat him, he's
our friend, we've just flown halfway around
the world to say hello."

The big dragon didn't care about their fire. He seemed to make himself even bigger. He was ready for a fight.

But so was Ziggy. And Arthur too.

Together they charged straight at the big dragon.

He might have been big, but he was slow too.

Arthur crash-landed on the top of his head.

Then Ziggy knocked him over with her tail.

The big dragon rolled around on the floor, squealing and groaning, then slunk into the back of the cave, head down, looking a bit ashamed.

I don't know how Ziggy and Arthur knew we were here. Or how they knew we needed help. I can't believe they could smell the chocolate all the way from Scotland. But they're definitely hungry. Ziggy just ate the last of the zblg.

Now Uncle Morton is scratching her ears in the way she likes best.

Arthur is curled up on my lap, half-asleep. He must be exhausted from the long journey.

The other dragons are watching us very carefully. I wouldn't be surprised if they'd still like to eat us. But they're not going to try. Not with Ziggy here to protect us.

Love from

Eddie

From: Edward Smith-Pickle

To: Mum

Date: Friday 13 April

Subject: The GDBC

 Attachments: Flying; Ceremony; Telescope; Wow!

Dear Mum

Today was the most amazing day of my life.

I saw the Great Dragon Battle Ceremony.

Actually, I didn't just see it. I took part in it!

When I woke up this morning, the dragons were gone. All except Arthur. He woke me up by flying into the air and crash-landing on my head. I could tell he wanted me to come outside.

Uncle Morton was still fast asleep. I thought it was best to leave him. He's not quite well yet. So I pulled on some clothes and followed Arthur out of the cave.

Ziggy was waiting there. She bent down her neck.

I knew what she meant. So I jumped aboard.
So did Arthur.

A moment later, we were flying through the
air.

Soon we were high above the mountains.
I've never seen such a beautiful view. About
a mile below me, I could see a shepherd. His
sheep were so tiny they looked like ants.

You'll be glad to hear I held on tight.

Suddenly I heard a great whooshing sound.

And a roaring.

Then the air filled with flames.

I thought we were being attacked. But actually I think the other dragon had just come to say hello.

Then another arrived. And another. And so many more that I couldn't even keep count.

There were dragons everywhere.

Flying in every direction.

Swooping. Diving. Looping-the-loop.

Doing the most amazing stunts.

It was like the greatest show on earth.

We had been zooming through the air for about twenty minutes when I happened to look down, and saw a tiny figure standing all alone in the snow.

At first I thought he was another shepherd. Then I realised he was watching the ceremony through a telescope.

I suddenly realised who he must be!

I tugged Ziggy's ear.

She didn't like that at all.

In fact, she tried to shake me off.

It's lucky she didn't, because I never would have survived such a long drop.

I held on tight and tugged her ear again. Then again. And about five more times before she finally understood what I meant. Then she plunged down to the ground and landed next to Professor Baast.

He recognised me immediately.

"You are being the Eddie!" he cried, and gave me a big hug.

His English isn't very good, but we managed to communicate quite well.

Apparently he has been here for about a week, waiting for the ceremony to begin.

Ziggy and Arthur went into the sky again and joined in with the ceremony. I stayed on the ground with Professor Baast and watched through his telescope.

We spent the rest of the day watching the Great Dragon Battle Ceremony.

Professor Baast counted the dragons. He said there were thirty-nine in total. Which is really quite a lot of dragons.

Some were huge. Others were tiny. There were a couple that were even smaller than Arthur.

All of them swooped and soared and dived, spitting fire and leaving trails of black smoke.

We still don't know what the ceremony means or why the dragons are doing it.

We do know one thing for sure. The ceremony isn't a battle, because none of them got hurt.

Maybe they were flying around for fun.

They certainly seemed to be enjoying themselves.

At the end of the day, we returned to the cave and found Uncle Morton. He was very sad to have missed the ceremony, but his head is better, so it's probably a good thing that he got such a long sleep.

Professor Baast doesn't know who the bones belong to. But they're obviously not his.

Love from

Eddie

From: Edward Smith-Pickle

To: Mum

Date: Saturday 14 April

Subject: Back in the village

Attachments: The Mongolian Air Force

Dear Mum

It took us seven days to climb the mountain on horseback. But flying down again only took about twenty minutes.

Ziggy gave us a lift on her back.

Professor Baast was a bit nervous. He said, "I am having the vertigo. Perhaps I am better for walking."

I told him not to worry. I fell off the horse three times this week, but I've never fallen off Ziggy.

"Is more far to fall," Professor Baast said, which is actually true.

In the end, he jumped on her back with me and Uncle Morton.

Ziggy flapped her wings. I told Professor Baast to hang on.

He said, "You don't worry, Eddie. I am very much hanging on."

You'll be glad to hear none of us fell off.

Professor Baast actually said it was the most exciting twenty minutes of his entire life.

When we landed in the middle of the village, everyone ran and hid.

Everyone except Bob.

He came running straight towards us with a huge grin on his face.

He hugged me. He hugged Uncle Morton. He hugged Professor Baast. He even hugged Ziggy, which was quite amazing, because you know how scared he is of dragons.

He said he thought he'd never see us again. Then he invited us into his yurt for lunch. I'm glad to say it wasn't zblg.

I hope you've got all my messages. I haven't had any back from you. Maybe Uncle Morton's phone hasn't been working properly.

I did just try calling you, but the reception is awful in this village. I'll try again later.

Love from

Eddie

Dear Uncle Morton

I have just eaten the best meal of my entire life: roast chicken and roast potatoes and peas followed by vanilla ice cream.

Mum and Gordon love their present. They say Mongolian cheese is delicious and why don't more people eat it in our country?

They even want to try zblg, so perhaps you could bring some when you come home.

Ziggy and Arthur are both fine.

They must be fast fliers, because they got home before me, and were waiting on your island when I arrived with a shopping bag full of food.

Everyone is fine at home too.

Mum said she was going to punish me for running away to Mongolia, but she hasn't yet.

I'm hoping she'll forget.

She still says she never wants to see you again, but she doesn't really mean it. She's just feeling a bit grumpy because Meg didn't sleep last night.

Love from

Eddie

Dear Eddie

I am so pleased to hear that your family are well. Thank you for looking after Ziggy and Arthur. I can't wait to see them – and your charming baby sister. She must already have grown enormously since I last saw her.

However, I shall not be returning to Scotland immediately. I am planning to spend a few more weeks in Mongolia. Professor Baast has asked me to accompany him back to the mountains to explore the dragons' cave again and discover exactly whose bones are inside.

We are currently buying equipment and supplies. Bob has promised to provide us with his best horses and camels. We will take enough chocolate to feed an army of dragons.

I don't know how long this expedition will take, but I may be some time. While I'm away, could you look after Ziggy and Arthur for me? As you know, they need nothing more than some nutritious food and the occasional tender scratch behind the ears.

With love from

your affectionate uncle

Morton

The Dragonsitter

Josh Lacey

Illustrated by Garry Parsons

Collect them all!

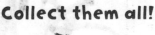